Shel
Silverstein

UNCLE SHELBY'S
STORY
OF

Lafcadio,

THE
LION
WHO
SHOT
BACK

HARPER & ROW, PUBLISHERS   NEW YORK, EVANSTON, AND

LONDON

LAFCADIO, THE LION WHO SHOT BACK

Even your old Uncle Shelby once had a teacher.

His name was Robert Cosbey.

This book is dedicated to him.

Lafcadio,

THE
LION
WHO
SHOT
BACK

And now, children, your Uncle Shelby is going to tell
you a story about a very strange lion—in fact, the strangest
lion I have ever met. Now, where shall I start this lion tail?
I mean this lion *tale*. I suppose that I should begin at the
moment that I first met this lion. Let's see . . . that was
in Chicago on Friday the 17th of December. I remember
very clearly because the snow had just started to turn
to slush and the traffic was very bad on Dorchester Avenue
and this lion was looking around for a barbershop and
I was just coming home from—

No, I suppose I should start this story long before that.
I suppose I should tell you about the lion when he was
very young. All right.

1.

Once there was a young lion and his name was—well,
I don't really know what his name was because he lived
in the jungle with a lot of other lions and if he did have
a name it certainly wasn't a name like Joe or Ernie
or anything like that. No, it was more of a lion name like,
oh, maybe Grograph or Ruggrrg or Grmmff or Grrrrr.

Well, anyway, he had a name like that and he lived in
the jungle with the other lions and he did the usual lion
things like jumping and playing in the grass and
swimming in the river and eating rabbits and chasing
other lions and sleeping in the sun, and he was very
happy.

Well, then, one day—I believe it was a Thursday—after all the lions had eaten a good lunch and were sleeping in the sun, snoring lions' snores, and the sky was blue and the birds were going kaw kaw and the grass was blowing in the breeze and it was quiet and wonderful, suddenly . . .

BLOWM!

There was such a loud sound, all the lions woke up fast
and jumped straight up in the air. And they started to run.
Lickety-split, lickety-clipt or clippety-clop, clippety-clop,
or is that the way horses run? Well, they ran
whatever way lions run. I don't know, maybe even
pippety-pat. Anyway, they all ran away—

Well, *almost* all.

There was one lion that did not run, and that is the one

I am going to tell you the story about. This one lion, he just sat up and blinked and winked in the sun and stretched his arms—well, maybe he stretched his paws—and he rubbed the sleep out of his eyes and he said, "Hey, why is everybody running?"

And an old lion who was running by said, "Run, kid, run, run, run, run, run, the hunters are coming."

"Hunters? Hunters? What are hunters?" said the young lion, still blinking in the sun.

"Look," said the old lion, "you'd better stop asking so many questions and just run if you know what's good for you."

So the young lion got up and stretched and began to run with the other lions. Pippity-pat, or was it clippety-clop? I think we have gone through all of this before.

"Hi, hunter," he said.

"Good heavens," cried the hunter, "a ferocious lion, a dangerous lion, a roaring, bloodthirsty man-eating lion."

"I am not a man-eating lion," said the young lion. "I eat rabbits and blackberries."

"No excuses," said the hunter. "I am going to shoot you."

"But I give up," said the young lion, and he put up his paws in the air.

"Don't be silly," said the hunter. "Who ever heard of a lion giving up. Lions don't give up, lions fight to the end. Lions eat up hunters! So I must shoot you now and make you into a nice rug and put you in front of my fireplace and on cold winter evenings I will sit on you and toast marshmallows."

"Well, my goodness, you don't have to shoot me," said the young lion. "I will be your rug and I will lie in front of your fireplace and I won't move a muscle and you can sit on me and toast all the marshmallows you want. I love marshmallows," said the young lion.

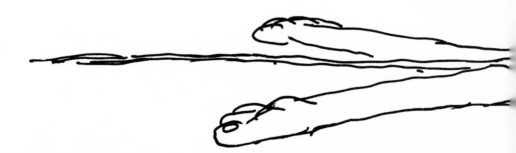

"You *what?*" said the hunter.

"Well," said the young lion, "to be absolutely honest with you, I don't know if I *really* love marshmallows or not because I have never tasted one, but I love most things and I love the *sound* of the word marshmallow and if they taste like they sound—mmmmmmmmmmmmm!—I just know I will love them."

"That's ridiculous," said the hunter. "I have never heard of a lion giving up. I have never heard of a lion eating marshmallows. I am going to shoot you now and that is that." And he put his funny stick up to his shoulder.

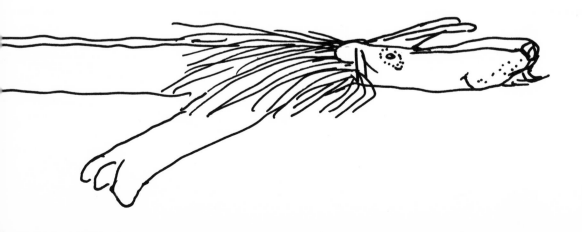

"But *why?*" said the young lion.

"Because *I am,* that is why," said the hunter, and he pulled the trigger. And the stick went click.

"What was that click?" said the young lion. "Am I shot?"

Well, as you can imagine, the hunter was very embarrassed about this and his face turned as red as his cap.

"I'm afraid I forgot to load my gun," he said. "I guess the joke is on me—ha ha—but if you will just excuse me for a moment, I will put a bullet in and we will go on from there."

"No," said the young lion, "I don't think I will. I don't think I will let you put a bullet in. I don't think I will let you shoot me. I don't think I want to be your rug and I don't think you are a very nice hunter after all and I think I am going to eat you up."

"But *why?*" said the hunter.

"Because *I am,* that's why," said the young lion.

And he did.

And after he had eaten the hunter all up, he ate the hunter's red cap, but it tasted sort of woolly. And after he had eaten up the red cap (Pooh! Doesn't it make your mouth feel funny to think about eating a red cap?), he tried to eat up the funny stick and the bullets, but he couldn't chew them, so he said, "Well, I guess I will keep these as a souvenir," and he picked them up in his teeth and he carried them back to the other lions.

2.

Now the other lions were all sitting around telling stories about who was the fastest in running away from the hunters and who was the bravest and who was the fiercest and other lies like that like lions like to lie about, and when the young lion walked up to them carrying the funny stick, they all jumped up and said, "Yoweee!" and "Yeee Yow!" and "Wow!" and "Where Did You Get That Gun?!!"

"Gun? Gun? What is a gun?"
asked the young lion.

"That is the stick they shoot us with," said the old
lion. "Now take it out of here and throw it away! It gives
me goose bumps just to look at it!" (Now wasn't that a silly
thing to say? Imagine a lion getting goose bumps. That is
almost as silly as a goose getting lion bumps.)

So the young lion sadly walked away with the gun in
his teeth.

"I wonder," said the young lion to himself, "I wonder
how they shoot this thing anyway?"

So he picked up a bullet in his teeth and he pushed it
into the gun with his nose and he shoved it into the barrel
with his tongue.

Then he stuck his left tooth into the trigger and tried
to shoot it, but he couldn't.

Then he stuck his right tooth into the trigger and tried
to shoot it, but he couldn't.

And then he tried to pick it up with his paws and shoot
it with his claws, which was even sillier, and he tried to
shoot it with his whiskers, and all he got out of that was
tired whiskers, and he stuck his tail into the trigger and
he pulled as hard as he could and the gun went

BAROOOM!

and all the other lions jumped up in the air again and started to run away.

"Hey," said the young lion, "stop running. It is only me and I have shot the gun."

Well, I tell you that when the other lions found out it was only the young lion making all that noise they were very angry.

"You had better forget about shooting," they said, "and stick to lioning where you belong."

But the young lion was very happy about shooting the gun, and do you know what he started to do?

Well, every afternoon while the other lions were sleeping, he would sneak away over the mountain and he would practice and practice and practice for hours and hours until finally one day he was able to lift the gun up in his paws.

And he practiced and practiced for days and days until finally he was able to shoot the gun but, of course, he wasn't able to hit anything except the sky.

And so he practiced and
practiced for weeks and weeks
until finally he was able to
hit the big mountain.

And he practiced and
practiced for months
and months until soon
he was able to shoot
the waterfall.

And soon he was able
to shoot the cliff.

And soon he was able to shoot the trees, and soon the coconuts off the trees, and then the berries off the bush, and then the flies off the berries, and then the ears off the flies, and the dust off the ears, and finally the sunlight off the dust.

And do you think he was a good shot?

Well, just the best in the world, that's all. Just the best shot in the whole world.

And what did he do for ammunition? Why, every time he ran out of bullets he just went out and ate up another hunter and took his bullets and went back and practiced some more.

3.

And then one nice day as he was practicing, the young lion heard some shooting from the other side of the jungle, and I don't have to tell you what happened. All the lions started running again.

"Where are you running?" asked the young lion.

"Look," said the old lion. "We have gone through all this before. You had just better stop asking so many questions and MOVE!"

So the young lion moved.
But after he had been
running for a while,
he stopped and he said
to himself, "Hey, why
am *I* running away?"

And he sat down right there in the middle of the jungle and began to shoot back at the hunters.

And suddenly, guess what? There were no more hunters left.

And after a while all the other lions came crawling
out of their hiding places and they couldn't believe their
eyes and they said, "Hey, what is going on around here
anyway?" and "Hey, what's happening?" and "Golly gee,"
and stuff like that, and they were all surprised and happy
and they all had lunch and then they lay down and slept

in the sun with smiles on their faces and little bits of
red wool on their whiskers.

And the young lion? Why he was the happiest of all
because he had piles and piles of new ammunition and
all the other lions said that he was the greatest lion that
they had ever seen, and they had seen plenty of lions.

So all the lions lived a very happy life and slept all

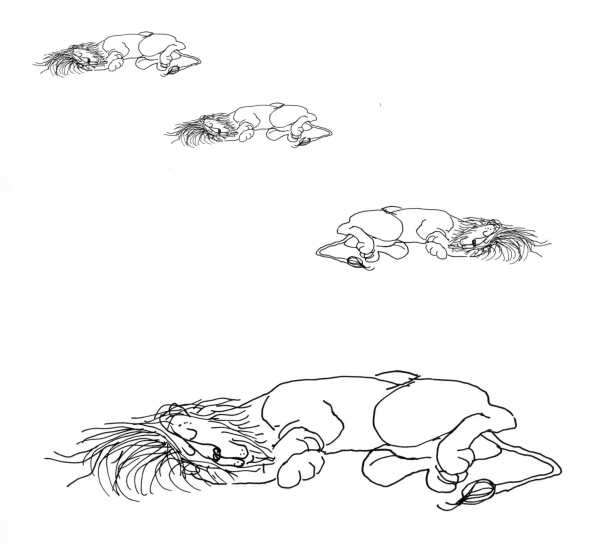

afternoon and played in the sun and floated in the river
and had a good time and never worried about anything,
because every time hunters came to shoot, why that
young lion shot right back at them, Boom Bum Bim Bim
Bam, until there were no more hunters left. And when
men came into the jungle to find out what happened to
the hunters, Bim Bam Boom—

Pretty soon there weren't any more of the "finder
outers" left.

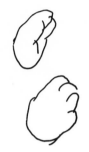

And when men came to find out about the finder outers, Boom Bam Bim—

Pretty soon there weren't any more of the finder outers about the finder outers left.

And pretty soon no men came into the jungle at all.

And it was nice and quiet.

And all the lions were fat and happy.

And all of them had nice hunter rugs.

4.

But then one rainy afternoon while the young lion was practicing some very fancy shooting—like standing on his head and shooting with his teeth and his toenails and his elbows with one eye closed and behind his back and sideways and even upside down— a little, fat bald-headed man came walking through the

jungle, and he had on a tall funny hat and an elegant
vest and a golden watch with a golden chain and shiny
shoes and he had a droopy mustache and a big fat belly that
shook when he laughed like a bowl full of raspberry jam
and he carried a gold-headed cane, and you could see that
he wasn't used to walking through the jungle because he
kept getting caught in the branches of the trees and he
kept tripping over roots and he kept stepping into puddles
and he kept saying, "Oh, me, oh, my," and "Ooee," and "Hey,
it *is* hot," and "Darned mosquitoes," and "Achoo," and
stuff like that.

Well, now, the lions didn't hear him coming until the
very last minute because, although lions have very good
ears and they can hear things from far off, if their ears are

washed that is, but if
their ears aren't washed,
they can't hear much
better than you can, and
to tell you the truth, I don't
think lions wash their ears
very often because washrags
are very hard to get in the
jungle and soap costs ten
cents and most lions don't
have ten cents and even if
they did they couldn't buy a
bar of soap because who
would sell a bar of soap to
a lion?

If a lion came knocking at
your door and had ten cents
in his paw and said,
"May I buy a bar of soap?"
would you sell him
a bar of soap?

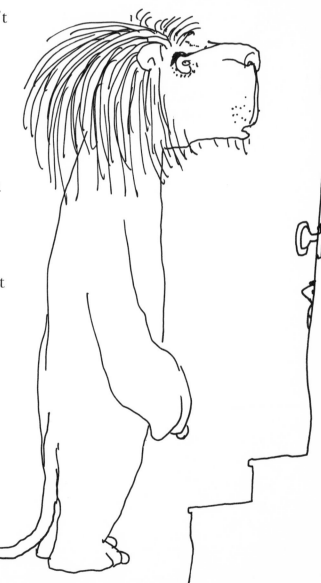

Well, so you can see why these lions didn't hear too well. But they saw him coming—and I'll tell you one thing, lions' eyes are always very good and they can see very well in the dark and it happened to be in the middle of the afternoon anyway and lions see extra-special well in the middle of the afternoon and you never see a lion wearing glasses, do you?

When the lions saw the little man coming, they didn't even bother to run—they just called out to the young lion:

"Hey, dinner is here!"

And then they rolled over and went back to sleep.

And the young lion, he just yawned and picked up his gun.

"I think I will shoot this one standing on my head with one eye crossed and three paws tied behind my back," he said, and he aimed his gun.

"Wait a minute, don't shoot me," cried the man.
And the young lion said, "Why not?"
And the man said, "Because I am not a hunter. I am
a circus man and I want you to come and be in my circus."
"Circus, shmircus, dominercus," said the young lion.
"I do not want to be in a cage in your old circus."

"You wouldn't have to
be in a cage," shouted
the circus man.
"You can be my trick
shooter."

"Shooter, shmooter, scooter,
booter," said the young
lion. "I am already a great
shooter. I am the
greatest shooter in
the jungle!" And he aimed
his gun again.

"But you can make lots
of money and you can
be the greatest shooter
in the world and you
can be famous and eat
wonderful foods and wear
silk shirts and yellow shoes
and smoke fifty-cent cigars

and go to wonderful parties and have everyone pat you on your back or scratch you behind the ears or whatever people do to lions; I don't know."

"Ears, shears, a glass of beers," said the young lion. "What do I want with all that stuff?"

"Everyone wants that stuff," said the circus man. "Come with me and be rich and famous and happy and be the greatest lion in all the world."

"Well," said the young lion, "if I do come, will I get a marshmallow?"

"A marshmallow?" said the circus man. waving his gold-headed cane and twirling the golden watch on a golden chain. "A marshmallow? Why, my good fellow, you will have thousands of marshmallows. You will have marshmallows for breakfast, marshmallows for lunch, and marshmallows for supper, and do you know what you will have between meals?"

"Marshmallows?" asked the young lion.

"Marshmallows!" shouted the circus man. "I will build you a marshmallow house and I will get you a marshmallow mattress for your bed for midnight snacks and I will make you a marshmallow suit with a marshmallow hat and when you take a shower you will take a shower with hot melted marshmallow. Why, you will have more marshmallows than any lion in the world. Shall I sing you the marshmallow song?"

Marshmallows Marshmallows
Marching Marshing Mellow
Malling Mallows Marshing Fellows
Marshy-Murshy—

"I'd rather you didn't," said the young lion.

"Well, it's really not too bad a song," said the circus man, "considering that I just made it up. Well, anyway, pick up your gun, pack up your suitcase, and let's go to to the big city."

"I don't have a suitcase," said the young lion.

"Too bad you aren't an elephant," said the circus man. "Because then you could pack up your *trunk*—ha ha ha ha."

"That is a pretty corny joke," said the young lion. "Even for the jungle."

"Hummpf," snorted the circus man. "Okay, pack up your toothbrush and let's get out of here."

"I don't have a toothbrush," said the young lion.

"No toothbrush?" said the circus man. "How do you brush your teeth?"

"I don't brush my teeth," said the young lion.

"You don't brush your teeth?" said the circus man. "What does your *dentist* say about that?"

"I don't *have* a dentist," said the young lion.

"You don't have a dentist?" said the circus man. "Well, then, who—"

"Look," said the young lion. "If you want to go, I will go. I will do anything rather than listen to all your terrible jokes."

So the circus man got on the lion's back and they
marched out of the jungle.

"You are sure about those marshmallows?" said the
young lion.

"Absolutely sure," said the circus man.

And away they went.

5.

Well, finally, after traveling
for many days and nights
they came to the city—and oh,
it wasn't anything at all like
the jungle. There were lots
of people and tall square
things and things that looked
like hippopotamuses that
moved very fast with people
inside them.

"What are those?" said the young lion.

"Those are cars," said the circus man.

"Can I have a car?" asked the young lion.

"Can you have a car?" said the circus man. "Why, you will have a car made of pure gold with silver wheels and diamond bumpers and marshmallow seats and . . ."

"Hey," said the young lion. "What are those tall, tall things with the windows in them?"

"Those are buildings," said the circus man. "Office buildings and apartment buildings and store buildings and school buildings and roller-skating rink buildings."

"Can I have a building?" asked the young lion.

"Can you have a building? Why, I'll get you the tallest, widest marshmallow building that you ever—"

And then the circus man yelled, "Taxi, taxi," and he waved his gold-headed cane and he whistled with his taxi whistle that hung from his watch chain, and a big taxi stopped.

"Take us to the Grumbacker Hotel," said the circus man.

"Wait a minute," said the taxi driver. "Is that lion with you?"

"Of course he is with me," said the circus man.

"Well, I am not taking no lion with me," said the taxi driver. (He couldn't speak English very well; if he could, he would have said "any.")

"No sir," he said, "I am not driving no lions around."

"GRAUGRRR," said the lion.

"Hop in, gentlemen," said the taxi driver with a big smile, and away they went.

6.

Now when they got to the hotel, they jumped out of the taxi and they went to get a room. "Give us a nice room with a nice bathtub," said the circus man to the hotel man.

"And a nice marshmallow bed," said the lion.

"Listen," said the hotel man. "You had better go somewhere else to get a room. This is a very fancy hotel and I don't want any lions living here!"

"GRAUGRRR," said the lion.

"Go right up to your room," said the hotel man, and they went into the elevator.

Now the young lion had never been in an elevator before because you know they don't have elevators in the jungle and he just loved the elevator, and when the elevator stopped and the elevator man said, "All out, fourteenth floor," the lion said, "Let's go up and down again! I want to go up and down again!"

"But this is your floor," said the elevator man. "You have to get out here."

GRAUGRRR

said the lion.

And so the poor elevator man had to drive the elevator up and down, up and down, until at last he felt very, very sick and said, "Please, please, can't we stop? I *hate* elevators!" And the young lion said,

GRAUGRRR

and the elevator man said, "Let's go up and down a few more times—I *love* elevators."

And finally, after everybody was very, very tired, the lion and the circus man got off the elevator and went to their room. And when they got inside, the circus man said, "Well, which side of the bed do you want?"

"It doesn't really make much difference to me," said the young lion. "I have never slept in any bed. I'll just sleep in the bushes if it's all the same to you."

"There are no bushes!" said the circus man.

"And besides, this nice bed is softer than any old sticky bushes. Why don't you lie down and try it?" So the young lion did.

"Doesn't that feel good?" said the circus man. "Isn't that nicer and softer than any old bushes?"

"Well," said the young lion, "it certainly is different!"

"Now come into the bathroom and take a nice hot bath," said the circus man. "You smell like an animal."

"Am I going to take a bath in nice melted marshmallow like you promised?" asked the young lion.

"Well, not right now," said the circus man. "We'll save that for later."

"Well, then," said the lion, "I guess I'll just take a bath in the river the way I have been doing."

"River?" asked the circus man. "There are no rivers running through hotel rooms! Why don't you just get into that nice bathtub full of hot water?"

"Don't you have to take your clothes off before you get into these things?" asked the young lion.

"Of course," said the circus man.

"Well," said the young lion, "I don't have any clothes to take off, so I guess I can't get into the tub."

"Nonsense," said the circus man, "you get right into that tub!"

And so the lion put one toe into the tub and he said,

"Yow, this is the *hottest* bathtub I have ever been in."

"This is the *only* bathtub you have ever been in" said the circus man.

"Isn't this much better than taking a bath in some dirty old river?"

And the lion just settled down into the hot water and said, "Well, it certainly tastes different, gulp, gulp!"

"Stop drinking that water," screamed the circus man. That is to wash with, not to drink."

"I am sorry," said the young lion, "but now I think I would really like my marshmallow."

"All in due time," said the circus man. "Right now we have to get you looking like a real gentleman sharpshooter —so please get out of that tub and get dried off."

So the young lion sighed and climbed out of the bathtub and got dried with a big white fluffy towel, and he dried off his claws and he dried off his mane and he even dried off the tip of his tail, which is very hard for a lion to dry, as you know.

7.

"Now," said the circus man, "you smell one hundred percent better. Now run down to the barbershop while I take a little nap. And also get some clothes to wear. We can't have you running around absolutely naked."

"Well, okay," said the lion. "But I've never really thought of myself as naked before!"

Now it took the young lion quite a while to get downstairs because he made the elevator man ride him up and down forty-six times, and when he finally got outside he began to look around for a barbershop. But he couldn't find one because he didn't know what a barbershop *looked* like. As a matter of fact, he didn't even know what a barbershop *was*. So he just walked around and looked for a barbershop while all the people just looked at him and said "Wow!" and "Yow!" and "ZOWIELOOKADALINE!" which means, "Zowie, look at the lion!"

And it was just about this time that your own Uncle Shelby was crossing the street on my way to get a hot dog with some tomato and onions on it, when the young lion walked up to me and said, "Excuse me, could you please direct me to a barbershop?"

Well, you can imagine how surprised I was to hear a lion ask me a question like that, but I said I would be glad to take him to an excellent barbershop, and he seemed very pleased.

"Thank you very much," he said. "You are the nicest person I have met since I have been in this country and you are also very, very handsome and very well dressed and you look like a man who is very intelligent and very kind. In fact," said the young lion, "I should think you would be President of the United States."

"No," I said, "I do not have time to be President of the

United States as I am too busy writing stories for children. But it is true that I am very handsome and very intelligent and very kind. I will admit to that."

So I took the young lion to the barbershop, but the barber was out to lunch and we just sat in the barber's chairs and chatted for a while, and I remember the lion had his claws manicured and he said he liked it very much although the woman who gave him the manicure said she had never seen such filthy nails in all her life.

Oh, my, how you would have laughed if you had seen him sitting there in that barber's chair with his long mane hanging down and his paws sticking out from under the sheet, getting a manicure. I'm only sorry you couldn't have seen him. As a matter of fact, I *did* see you walking past the barbershop with your mother just about that time, and I tapped on the window but I guess you didn't hear me because you were looking at a fire engine and you didn't even turn around.

"Would you like a shoeshine?" asked the shoeshine boy.

"As a matter of fact I would, but I don't have any shoes," said the lion.

"Well, then, how about a paw shine?" asked the shoeshine boy.

"Yes," said the young lion, "I think I would like a paw

shine very much." So the lion had his paws shined and he was very pleased with them and he asked me if I didn't think they looked very beautiful and shiny and I said yes, but to tell you the truth I didn't think his paws looked much different from before they were shined, but I didn't want to hurt his feelings. And finally the barber came back from lunch. "Oh, my gosh," said the barber, "I must have eaten a terrible lunch. I should never have had that chocolate ice cream mixed in with my corned beef hash because now I have got indigestion and I think I am seeing things. As a matter of fact, I think I see a lion in my barber chair having his paws shined and his claws manicured."

"No," I said, "you are not seeing things. This is my friend the lion and he wants a haircut and I imagine he wants his mustache trimmed also."

"Yes," said the lion, "I want a very good haircut. That is the main thing!"

"Well, you won't get it here," said the barber, "I don't cut lions' hair."

"GRAUGRRR," said the lion.

"Yes, sir!" said the barber, with a great big smile.
And the lion got his haircut!

And then the barber gave him a massage, which he loved very much (because that is very much like being scratched behind the ears); and he had his head sprinkled with water that smelled wonderful, and he loved that part best of all; and as a matter of fact he drank up half a bottle of it before I could tell him that that was definitely *not* the thing to do!

And finally the young lion got out of the barber's chair and smiled and said, "Let's go, Uncle Shelby, I feel like a new lion!"

"Just a minute," said the barber, "you haven't paid me yet and that will cost you exactly . . ."

GRAUGRRR

said the lion.

"Exactly *nothing*," said the barber, smiling. "Today is the day I am giving free haircuts and I hope you enjoyed yours very much."

8.

Now it was just about five o'clock when your Uncle Shelby came out of the barbershop with the lion, and I noticed that that lion was looking at me in a hungry sort of way so I said, "How about having a bite of supper with me?"

And the lion said that he wouldn't mind.

So I took him to a very nice little restaurant over on 57th Street.

"I think you will like the food here," the waiter said, as we sat down. "Everything is quite delicious—"

"Well," said the lion, "it doesn't look so good to me but—well—if you say so—"

"Stop, stop," cried the waiter, "you're eating up the menu!"

"Oh, my," said the lion, "I'm sorry, but you said that everything was delicious so—"

"My dear lion," the waiter said, "I was speaking only of the food. The menus here are not too tasty at all, and also, I might add, eating a menu is not at all good taste."

"Maybe not," said the lion, "but it is still better manners than eating up a waiter."

"I guess he's right there," said the waiter with a big smile. "But now, gentlemen, how about some nice lamb chops with a baked potato and some string beans and then some chocolate pudding with—"

"I want a marshmallow," said the young lion.

"A marshmallow?" said the waiter. "We don't serve marshmallows here; this is a very fancy restaur—"

GRAUGRRR

said the lion.

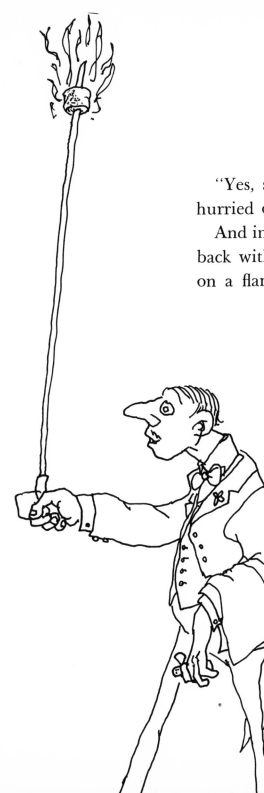

"Yes, sir," said the waiter, and he
hurried off to the kitchen.

And in a few moments he came
back with a beautiful marshmallow
on a flaming sword.

"Ah!" said the lion. "A marshmallow at last, at last a marshmallow, at mast a larshmellow." You can see how nervous and excited he was.

And he picked up the marshmallow. "It's as light as a feather," he said.

And he put the marshmallow on his tongue. "Ooh, it's crispy on the outside," he said.

And he bit into it with his big teeth. "Ooh, it's creamy on the inside," he said.

And he chewed it up.

"Oh," he said, and he closed his eyes and smiled.

And he swallowed it.

"It's delicious," he said. "It's better than rabbits any time."

"More marshmallows," cried the lion. "More, more, more, more marshmallows."

"Yes, sir," said the waiter, and he hurried off and he brought the lion a whole platter of marshmallows.

"Delicious," said the lion. "More marshmallows." And the waiter brought him a southern-fried marshmallow.

"Wonderful," said the lion.

And he brought him a marshmallow in tomato sauce.

"Scrumptious," said the lion.

And he brought him a boiled marshmallow and a scrambled marshmallow and a poached marshmallow and marshmalloup (which is a marshmallow soup) and marshmallops (which are marshmallow chops) and marshmallew (which is marshmallow stew) and a marshmomlette (which is a marshmallow omelette) and marshmeverything!

And do you know what the lion ate for dessert?

Wrong!

He ate his napkin.

Ha! Ha! That's a good joke on you!

And finally the young lion leaned back in his chair and patted his stomach.

"I feel wonderful," he said, and he smiled and wiped his mouth with his tail.

"Now I must have a suit—a gentleman-shooter's suit! Tell me, Uncle Shelby, do you know of a good tailor?"

"A good tailor? My boy," I said, "your old Uncle Shelby is the best dressed man in this city and possibly the world. I will take you to my own personal tailor and he will make you the most beautiful suit that any lion ever had."

And so the young lion and your Uncle Shelby walked arm in arm to the tailor shop on Taylor Street.
And we went inside and there were the tailor and the tailor's assistant, and the tailor's assistant's assistant.

"Hi, tailors," said the lion. "Make me a beautiful suit!"

"A suit for a lion?" said the tailor. "Definitely not!"

"Absolutely not!" said the tailor's assistant.

"Absoposidefinitely not!" said the tailor's assistant's assistant.

GRAUGRRR

said the lion.

"Yes, sir," said the tailor.

"Oh, definitely," said the tailor's assistant.

"Oh, defiposolutely!" said the tailor's assistant's assistant.

"How about a nice brown tweed suit?" said the tailor.

"How about a lovely blue gabardine suit?" said the tailor's assistant.

"How about a beautiful purple and yellow suit with

red polka dots and a vest to match?" said the tailor's
assistant's assistant!

    And the lion tried on some suits.

    "I don't like them," said the lion.

"How about a nice white marshmallow suit?" said the lion.

"A marshmallow suit? Why, that's silly. You can't make a suit out of marshmallows!"

"GRAUGRRR," said the lion.

"Yes, sir!" said the tailor.

"Oh, definitely yes!" said the tailor's assistant.

And the tailor's assistant's assistant didn't say anything because he was already down at the candy store buying up all the marshmallows he could find.

And after a while he came back with a whole load of marshmallows, and the three tailors put their heads together and tried to figure out a way to make a marshmallow suit.

Now, first they tried to sew
it with a needle and thread,
but that didn't work.

And then they tried to sew it on the sewing machine, but the sewing machine got all gummed up with marshmallow.

And then the tailor's assistant's assistant got an idea, so they stuck the marshmallows together with raspberry jam and made the suit. And they showed it to the lion.

"How does it look?" they asked.

"Dee-licious!" said the lion, and he put it on—and you should have seen him: A big lion's head sticking out of a suit of marshmallows. And he looked at himself in the mirror.

"Wonderful," said the lion. "Now I really am a dandy lion . . . except it looks just a bit lumpy! Maybe you'd better iron the wrinkles out."

"But you can't iron marshmallows," said the tailor. "Marshmallows will—"

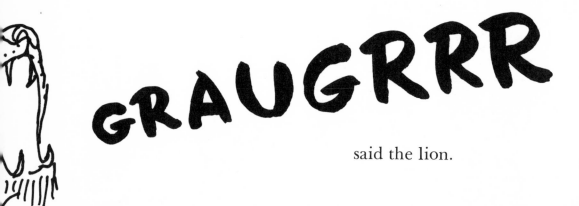

GRAUGRRR

said the lion.

And the tailor's assistant brought an iron and they began ironing out the marshmallow suit—right on the lion. And do you know what happened? Of course you do. The marshmallows melted all over the lion until he was covered from head to toe to tail with sticky icky drippy runny gummy gooey goopy melted marshmallows!

And the marshmallows dripped into his eyes and he couldn't see and they dripped into his ears and he couldn't hear and they dripped into his mouth, which he liked very much. And your good old Uncle Shelby had to lead the poor lion out of the tailor shop and back to the hotel to get him a hot bath as quickly as possible.

And let me tell you that the tailor and the tailor's assistant and the tailor's assistant's assistant seemed very happy to see us go. And I believe that they are still a bit angry with me for bringing a lion into their shop to buy a marshmallow suit.

9.

Well, we finally got to the hotel and after we had gone
up and down in the elevator twenty-eight times, we went
to meet the circus man, and he made the young lion take
another bath to get all the marshmallow off and then he
asked me if I would stay for a glass of buttermilk and I
said, "Yes, I will."

So the lion and the circus man and I sat around until
very late drinking buttermilk and telling jokes and
smoking big black cigars and singing the marshmallow song,

which is really not too bad a song once you've had a few glasses of buttermilk.

"Well, I think we had all better get a good night's sleep," said the circus man finally, "because tomorrow things are really going to start popping for Lafcadio the Great, the star of the Finchfinger Circus."

"Who is Finchfinger?" asked the young lion.

"That is I," said the circus man.

"And who is Lafcadio the Great?" asked the lion.

"That is *you*," said the circus man.

"But my name is Grummfgff or Mmmff, or something like that," said the young lion.

"Don't be silly," said the circus man. "You can't say Grummfgff the Great, or Mmmff the Great, or Something-Like-That the Great—from now on your name is Lafcadio and let me tell you, Lafcadio the Great, that tomorrow morning things are really going to start popping for you!"

Well, let me tell you old Finchfinger wasn't just kidding. The very next morning there was a great big parade for Lafcadio the Great all the way from the hotel to the circus tent and the band was playing and the sun was shining and Lafcadio the Great was riding in a big golden convertible and the band was playing *Umpa Umpa Umpa* and the people were cheering *"Hurrah, Hurrah!"* and "Yea, hey, hurray" and "Whoopie" and "Wow" and "Two, four, six, eight, who do we appreciate? Lafcadio, Lafcadio, Lafcadio the Great, yea!" And they threw confetti at Lafcadio, who was so happy that he smiled at everybody and opened his mouth and caught some of the confetti and ate it and everybody

cheered and he waved his tail all around and curled his mustache and he honked the horn on the car, *honk, honk,* and the band played *Ompa Ompa Ompa Boom* and *Boom, Appa, Appa, Ompa, Ompa,* and the crowd kept yelling "Yea, hey, hurray," and Lafcadio the Great was the happiest lion in all the world.

Of course your Uncle Shelby was invited to ride in the parade, but if you want to know, my alarm clock didn't go off and by the time I got up and had my breakfast of two soft-boiled eggs with small sausages and white-bread toast and jelly, why the parade was all over and thousands of people were already in the circus tent waiting for Lafcadio the Great.

And the band played *Ompa Ompa Boom Boom,* and the drums rolled.

And finally, the ringmaster with the long mustache hollered:

"Ladies and Gentlemen, presenting the only sharpshooting lion in the world, Lafcadio the Great!"

And everyone went "Hooray, Hooray" and Lafcadio the Great came out—and he was wearing a brand-new white suit that Mr. Finchfinger had bought for him and a big yellow cowboy hat and yellow boots and he had a brand-new silver gun with a pearl handle and a diamond-studded holster with lots of bullets made of pure gold, and he waved and he picked up his gun and first he shot six bottles off the table, *bang, bang, bang, bang, bang, bang.*

And then he shot a hundred balloons off the ceiling *bang, bang, bang, bang, bang, bang, bang, bang*

(you can put in the other ninety-two bangs
yourself); and then he told everybody in the circus
to put a marshmallow on his head and he shot the
marshmallows off everybody's head in the circus including
all the kids and a few of the monkeys.

And then he told everybody in the audience to hold
up the ace of spades and he shot every card in the

middle—12,322 of them (but he did it with 12,323 shots because he missed once), and the people went *"Hurrah," "Hurrah," "Hurrah."*

And then he shot between his legs and he shot under his arms and standing on his head, and he shot lying on his side and sitting on his hands and he shot rolling over and he never missed once after that and the people began to shout *"Rah! Rah! Rah! Lafcadio the Great is the greatest shot in the world."*

And he was.

And that was how LAFCADIO THE GREAT JOINED THE CIRCUS.

And from that day on I saw very little of Lafcadio the Great. Because everybody knows he was busy traveling with the circus from city to city, from New York to Racine to St. Paul doing trick shots for millions of kids and men and women.

And Lafcadio the Great began to get more famous and more famous until everybody in America knew about him.

And he went over to London to shoot for the Queen.

And he went to Paris to shoot for the Prime Minister.

And he went to Iran to shoot for the Shah.

And he went to Russia to shoot for the Premier.

And he went to Yugoslavia to shoot for the Marshal.

And he even went to Washington to shoot for the President.

And he became very, very rich, and now and then I would get a letter from him telling me he had just had tea with the Prince of Wales or that he had just been sailing in Bermuda or that he had just met a beautiful movie actress, and stuff like that.

And after a while I would just get a picture postcard from him showing the Eiffel Tower or the Sahara Desert or the Ellis Memorial Library of East Rockford, Illinois. And it would say, "Having a good time" or "Wish you were here" or just "Hi."

And of course Lafcadio learned many things he had never learned before. He learned to sign autographs because he was so famous that everyone wanted his autograph, and everyone was especially delighted with him because he would sign six autographs at once: two with his front paws and two with his back paws and one with his tail and one with his teeth.

But after a while of course he would sign only one
at a time with his right front paw because that was more
like a man and less like a lion and Lafcadio was becoming
more and more like a man all the time. For instance, he
stood on his back paws and he learned to sit at the table with
his left hand in his lap and his elbows off the table.

And he stopped eating menus.

And he learned to wear dark suits and white shirts
with button-down collars and tweedy brown suits
with plaid shirts and turned-up collars.

And he learned to wear collars with starch in them.

And then he learned to wear collars with *no* starch in
them.

And he kept his tail curled up and seldom let it hang
down except when he forgot himself or he had a little
too much buttermilk to drink.

And often I would see him
dancing in nightclubs with
the most beautiful, beautiful girls.

"Hi, Lafcadio," I would say.

"Hi, Uncle Shelby," he would
answer. "Come on over to my
table and have a little buttermilk."

And I would, and he would
talk about old times when
Lafcadio didn't even know
what a barbershop was.

And as time went by,
Lafcadio the Great became
greater and greater and
his picture was in all the
newspapers.

And Lafcadio the Great
became more and more
like a man.

And he began to play golf.

And he began to play tennis.

And he went swimming and diving.

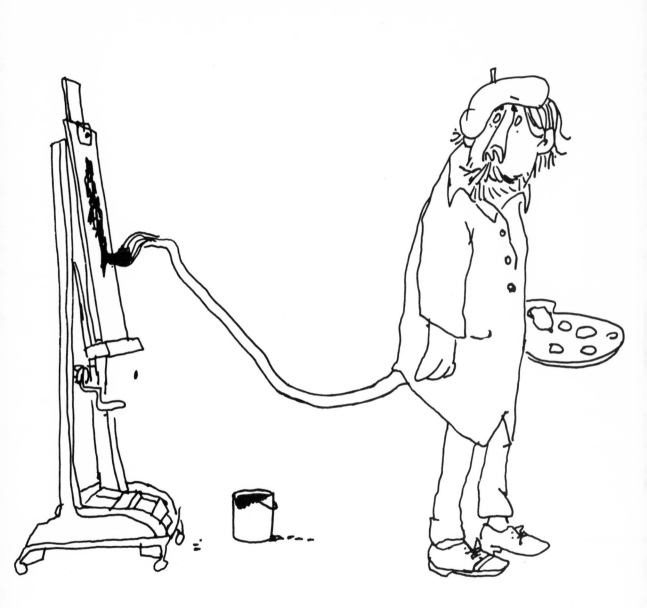

And he began to paint pictures (but to tell you the truth he couldn't draw a straight lion, ha ha).

And he did
exercises to
stay in shape.

And he went skating.

And he almost learned to ride a bicycle.

And he spent his vacations lying on the beach at
Cannes.

And he learned to sing and play the guitar.
And he learned to bowl.

And he seldom said "GRAUGRRR" except on very
special occasions, and everyone wanted him at
parties.

And he became a social lion.

And he wrote his autobiography. And everybody bought it.

And he became a literary lion.

And he had his clothes made to order—just so!

And he became a clothes lion.

And I suppose he was just about as happy and rich and famous as anyone could ever hope to be.

10.

And then, one day, just as your old Uncle Shelby had finished his supper and was about to settle down in his easy chair with his pipe and slippers and hot chocolate and his *National Geographic* magazines, the telephone rang.

"Hello, Uncle Shelby, this is Lafcadio the Great. Can you come to my house immediately? I need your advice because you are the wisest man in all the world!"

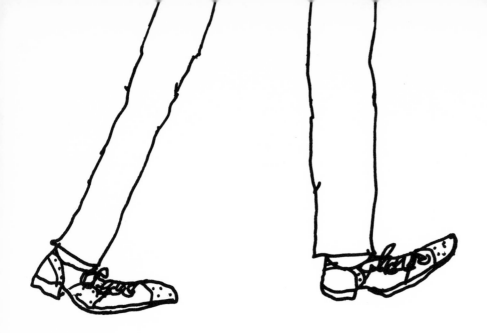

"Of course I'll come," I said. "I have never yet let
down a friend in trouble." And so I dressed in a hurry
and went out into the night which was 65 below zero,
and I remember I couldn't get a taxicab and so I had to
walk the twelve miles in the snow and it took me fifteen
minutes because the snow was very deep and I forgot my
galoshes. And when I got to Lafcadio's castle the butler
showed me in through the hallway, which was made of
silver, and through the dining room, which was made of
platinum, and into the study, which was made of gold,
and there was Lafcadio the Great—and do you know
what he was doing?

He was crying.

"Why are you crying, my friend?" I asked. "You have
money and you are famous and you have seven big cars
and you are loved by everyone and you are the greatest
shot in all the world. Why are you crying—you have
everything!"

"Everything isn't everything," said Lafcadio the
Great, dripping big tears down on the golden rug.

"I'm tired of my money and my fancy clothes.

"I'm tired of eating Rock Cornish hen stuffed with rice.

"I'm tired of going to parties and dancing the cha-cha
and drinking buttermilk.

"And I'm tired of smoking five-dollar cigars and playing
tennis and I'm tired of signing autographs and I'm tired
of *everything!* I want to do something *new!*"

"Something new?" I asked.

"Something *new!*" he said. "But there isn't anything
new to *do!*"

And he started to cry again.

Now, I could never stand to see anyone cry, so I said,
"Have you tried going up and down the elevator a few
times?"

"This morning I went up and down the elevator
1,423 times. IT'S OLD STUFF!" and he started to cry again.

"Have you tried a few more marshmallows?" I asked.

"So far I've eaten 23,241,562 marshmallows," said the
lion. "And I'm tired of them too! I want something
NEW!"

And he put his head down and began to cry some
more.

And just then the door banged open and in rushed
Finchfinger the circus man, waving his cane. "Hi-ho,
Lafcadio the Great," he shouted. "Stop crying and start
smiling, because every cloud must have a silver lioning and
I have just thought of a new wonderful thing to do. And
it's brand-*NEW!*"

"What is that?" Lafcadio the Great sniffed, looking
up with great big tears running down his nose.

"Hunting," said the circus man. "We are going to
Africa on a hunting trip, so pack your guns and your
suitcase and let's get going."

"Wonderful," said Lafcadio the Great. "I have never
been on a hunting trip. Come on, Uncle Shelby, pack
your bags and come too! We'll have a wonderful time!"

"Well, I would just love to go," I said, "but there is
no one here to water my philodendron plant while I'm
away, so I will have to stay here. But do write me and let
me know if you are having a good time."

So Lafcadio the Great
packed up his suitcases
and his guns and he and
Finchfinger and lots of
other hunters went to Africa
to do a little hunting.

11.

And when they got to Africa they put on their red
caps and they picked up their guns and they went into
the jungle and they all began shooting at some lions,
when suddenly one very, very old lion looked closely at
Lafcadio and said, "Hey, wait a minute, don't I know you?"

"I don't think so," said Lafcadio.

"Well, how come you are shooting at us?" asked the old, old lion.

"Because you are a lion and I am a hunter," said Lafcadio. "That's why."

"You are not a hunter," said the old lion, looking at him even closer. "You are a *lion*. I can see your tail sticking out from under your jacket. You are definitely a lion."

"Dear me," said Lafcadio, "dear me, so I am; I had almost completely forgotten about it."

"What is going on there, Lafcadio?" said the hunters. "Stop talking to those lions and start shooting those lions."

"Don't listen to him," said the old lion. "You are a lion just like us. Help us, and after we finish with these hunters we'll all go back into the jungle and sleep in the sun and swim in the river and play in the tall grass and eat some nice raw rabbits and have a wonderful time."

"Raw rabbits!" said Lafcadio. "Aarrgh ptu!"

"Don't listen to him," said the hunters. "You are a man just like us. Help us, and after we finish with these lions we'll sail back to America and go to some wonderful parties and play badminton and drink buttermilk and have a wonderful time."

"Buttermilk!" said Lafcadio. "Aarrgh ptu!"

"Well," said the man, "if you are a man, you had better help us shoot these lions, because if you are a lion we certainly are going to shoot you."

"Well," said the old, old lion, "if you are a lion you had better help us eat up those men, because if you are a man we are certainly going to eat you up. So make up your mind, Grmmff."

"Make up your mind, Lafcadio,"
said the man.

"Make up your mind," they
all said together, and poor
Lafcadio the Great, he couldn't
make up his mind; he
wasn't really a lion anymore
and he certainly wasn't
really a man.

Poor, poor Lafcadio—what do you do when you don't want to be a hunter—and you don't want to be a lion?

"Look," he said, "I don't want to shoot any lions, and I certainly don't want to eat up any of you hunters. I don't want to stay here in the jungle and eat raw rabbits and I certainly don't want to go back to the city and drink buttermilk. I don't want to chase my tail, but I don't want to play bridge either. I guess I don't belong in the hunter's world and I guess I don't belong in the lion's world. I guess I just don't belong anywhere," he said.

And with that he shook his head and he put down his gun and he picked up his hat and he sniffled a couple of times and he walked away over the hill, away from the hunters and away from the lions.

And he walked and walked, and soon from far away he could hear the sound of the hunters shooting the lions and he could hear the sound of the lions eating up the hunters.

And he didn't really know where he was going, but he did know he was going somewhere, because you really have to go somewhere, don't you?

And he didn't really know what was going to happen
to him, but he did know that something was going to
happen, because something always does, doesn't it?

And the sun was just beginning to go down behind
the hill and it was getting a little chilly in the jungle and
a warm rain was beginning to fall and Lafcadio the Great
walked down into the valley alone.

And that was the last I ever heard of Lafcadio the Great.

I certainly thought that he would have at least dropped me a line to say hello or maybe even sent me a little something for my birthday (which is September 25th in case any of you sweet children care to know).

But so far not a word from him.

And not a word about him either.

Of course, if I do get any news of him, I'll be sure to let you know. And who knows? You may even meet him before I do—

Maybe on your way to school, or maybe in the movies, or maybe in the park, or maybe in an elevator, or maybe in the barbershop, or maybe just walking down the street.

Maybe even down at the store, buying five or six dozen boxes of marshmallows.

He just loves marshmallows!